PROFILES

Cardinal Basil Hume

Gerard Noel

Illustrated by
Nicholas Day

Hamish Hamilton
London

Titles in the Profiles *series*

Muhammad Ali	0-241-10600-1
Chris Bonington	0-241-11044-0
Ian Botham	0-241-11031-9
Geoffrey Boycott	0-241-10712-1
Charlie Chaplin	0-241-10479-3
Winston Churchill	0-241-10482-3
Sebastian Coe	0-241-10848-9
Roald Dahl	0-241-11043-2
Thomas Edison	0-241-10713-X
Queen Elizabeth II	0-241-10850-0
The Queen Mother	0-241-11030-0
Alexander Fleming	0-241-11203-6
Anne Frank	0-241-11294-X
Gandhi	0-241-11166-8
Basil Hume	0-241-11204-4
Kevin Keegan	0-241-10594-3
Helen Keller	0-241-11295-8
Martin Luther King	0-241-10931-0
Paul McCartney	0-241-10930-2
Lord Mountbatten	0-241-10593-5
Rudolf Nureyev	0-241-10849-7
Pope John Paul II	0-241-10711-3
Anna Pavlova	0-241-10481-5
Prince Philip	0-241-11167-6
Lucinda Prior-Palmer	0-241-10710-5
Barry Sheene	0-241-10851-9
Mother Teresa	0-241-10933-7
Margaret Thatcher	0-241-10596-X
Daley Thompson	0-241-10932-9
Queen Victoria	0-241-10480-7

First published 1984 by
Hamish Hamilton Children's Books
Garden House, 57-59 Long Acre, London WC2E 9JZ
© 1984 text by Gerard Noel
© 1984 illustrations by Nicholas Day
British Library Cataloguing in Publication Data
Noel, Gerard
Basil Hume. — (Profiles)
1. Hume, George Basil — Juvenile literature
2. Cardinals — England — Biography —
Juvenile literature
I. Title   II. Series
282'.092'4   BX4705.H82/
ISBN 0-241-11204-4
Typeset by Pioneer
Printed in Great Britain at the
University Press, Cambridge

Contents

The publishers would like to apologise to Nicholas Day for wrongly
attributing the illustrations to E. Mortlemans on the back cover of the book.

Cardinal Basil Hume was the fourth Abbot of Ampleforth from 1963 to 1976

1 A Visit to Archbishop's House

When you think of an Abbot, you probably think of an important-looking man of the Church wearing elaborate vestments. On his head is a mitre — a tall, ornate cap with peaks at front and back. In his right hand he holds a crozier, which is a decorative version of a shepherd's crook. This is a sign that an Abbot, like a Bishop, has a 'pastoral' role and is supposed to tend to the 'sheep' of his flock with as much care as a loving shepherd.

An even more important churchman is a Cardinal, a title that exists only in the Roman Catholic Church, and which dates back to about the year A.D.500. In due course the Cardinals became very grand and were known as Princes of the Church. Their formal robes were, and still are of brilliant scarlet, and in days gone by they used to add long trains to their clothing on ceremonial occasions.

All these outward trappings have now been greatly simplified throughout the Roman Catholic Church. All you would need to do to see how much things have changed would be to go and visit a tall, lanky and relaxed man of just over sixty (though he looks much less) in his home at Archbishop's House, behind Westminster Cathedral in London. His name is George

9

Basil Hume, who was once an Abbot and is now a Cardinal. He was made a Cardinal when, in 1976, he became the most important person in the Catholic Church in England and Wales by becoming Archbishop of Westminster.

*   *   *

So let's imagine that you are visiting the Cardinal at Archbishop's House. He receives quite a lot of visitors there every day. You might be on your own, or with a parent, aunt or friend. Perhaps you have come to discuss some family matter or a school problem. Whatever the reason, you will be made very welcome, even though you might find the moment of standing at the large front door a bit unnerving. But then visits to big houses where important people live always are a bit frightening. Quite soon a friendly face will appear at the door and you will immediately be taken up a wide flight of stairs and into a reception room. This is a large but cosy room with a comfortable sofa and two deep armchairs arranged around a welcoming fireplace. After a couple of minutes, in will come the Cardinal. It is at this point that you might get a shock.

There are no scarlet robes, nor even a scarlet skull cap, which Cardinals often wear. Cardinal Hume will just be wearing a plain and, if he will forgive my saying so, probably rather crumpled-looking black suit: or, just as likely, an old pair of black trousers and a black or grey jersey. These are his working clothes when at home and if you are a close friend he will naturally not bother to dress up. The only sign that he is a priest will be his Roman collar and, possibly, a plain cross around

10

his neck. It is interesting to note that he is the first Archbishop of Westminster not to wear formal clothes on almost every occasion. If you had visited Cardinal Hume's predecessor, Cardinal Heenan, for example, he would certainly have been wearing a black cassock with scarlet buttons and a scarlet sash.

But the Cardinal does not dress casually because he is lazy or because he wants to make an effect. It is simply that Basil Hume is one of the most natural people you could ever wish to meet. He wears the right sort of clothes for the right occasion, and would never dream of trying to impress anyone. Knowing this should help to put you at your ease as you sit down on one of the comfortable chairs while the Cardinal offers you some tea, coffee, or lemonade. Then as he sits down and stretches out his long legs, you will notice how tall he is. His most prominent features are his slightly sticking-out ears, his long nose and the shock of wiry-looking white hair, a lock of which usually dangles over his forehead. He often jokes about his ears or nose and they are of course a boon to people who draw cartoons and caricatures of him.

If you have come to ask the Cardinal his opinion or advice about something, he will listen with great attention and then give an unhurried reply in a chatty, friendly way. You will probably feel able to chip in at any time because, within moments of having met him, nearly everyone feels they are having a chat with an affectionate uncle or old friend, rather than with a 'Prince of the Church'.

*   *   *

I give this example in starting off this short book about Cardinal Hume because such visits, by all sorts of people, take up quite a lot of his time and form an important part of his work. In the eight years since he has been at Westminster, hundreds of visitors have sat where you in your imagination are now sitting, telling him their news and being aware of his undivided attention and interest. Talking to him is, above all, not a frightening experience. He is not a frightening person, but a comforting one. He has a gift for putting people at their ease and so helping them to sort out their own thoughts. Over the years, this gift has helped him to be a guide on spiritual and other matters for which thousands have had great cause for gratitude.

Cardinal Hume has had a lot of experience in trying to help others, especially young people, as he was a teacher for a long time in his earlier days. But, as he has said himself, he was a teacher who learned as much from the young people around him as they ever learned from him. He put this knowledge to use when he was elected Abbot of his monastery (that is the leader of the community of Benedictine monks to which he belonged at Ampleforth Abbey in Yorkshire). He found it more useful still when called upon to become leader of an even larger and very different sort of community, namely the 'archdiocese' of Westminster, which takes in all of London north of the Thames and much surrounding territory as well.

As you leave Archbishop's House after your visit to Cardinal Hume, he will almost certainly make a point of seeing you down to the front door, chatting away pleasantly and giving you the chance to remember some last point you may have forgotten. This is a habit he continued even when he was still limping very badly after a hip operation at the beginning of 1983. He had suffered from arthritis for several years, a hard burden for a man who had been very active all his life and also a keen and successful athlete. Keeping himself fit has always been, and still is, something the Cardinal considers very important. It is in fact essential for the hard job he does and the long hours of work he puts in — all of which he does in a way that makes it look easy. Even at big ceremonies, official banquets or mass meetings, he looks and acts exactly as he did during that imaginary interview just described: totally natural, remarkably unassuming and yet quite obviously possessing great wisdom and quiet but distinct authority.

It has been said that the Cardinal is a complicated man, but this is largely because he is so often called upon to tackle complicated problems. He does this by first reducing the problems to their core and working on them from there, always with a great awareness, as he firmly believes, that God comes into the question at every stage. For Cardinal Hume is a man of prayer. But do not imagine him spending hours on his knees rooted to the spot and reciting set words. He looks on prayer — about which he has spoken and written much of great interest — rather as he looks on conversation with a friend. He feels a relaxed intimacy with God to whom he can 'listen' as well as talk in an easy, unaffected manner. But he did not learn to do this overnight. The secret of how he has come to manage it is one of the many fascinating things that can be found out by looking more closely at his life.

2 The Humes of Newcastle

Basil Hume is the name by which the Cardinal Archbishop of Westminster is best known, but it is not the name with which he was christened. He only took the extra 'religious' name of Basil years later when he became a Benedictine monk. At his christening he was given the name George, having been born on 2 March 1923 at Newcastle-on-Tyne.

His home was a secure and happy one. And, as such, it was very different from that of the majority of Catholic families who lived in the Tyneside area in the twenties, most of whom were of Irish origin and very poor. These Catholics made up the second and third waves of people forced by poverty to leave Ireland during the second half of the nineteenth century. (The first to arrive had mostly settled around Liverpool and Manchester.) To be poor was of course not unusual in those days, and poverty was well-known too among the Geordies. The time after the First World War and through the thirties was one of great hardship for working people, particularly in coal-mining areas such as Northumberland and Durham. (Newcastle-on-Tyne was then in the county of Northumberland which has since been divided so that the city is now in the newly-named county of Tyne and Wear.)

15

Newcastle-upon-Tyne — Cardinal Hume's birthplace

But the Hume family was neither Irish nor poor. And it was unusual too because the parents were of different religions. In those days there were fewer 'mixed marriages' than there are today. In other words, Catholics tended to marry other Catholics. As their numbers were relatively small, they usually stuck together to keep their religion strong. But nowadays there are many more Catholics in England and 'mixed marriages' are less rare.

Basil Hume's father was a Scotsman from just north of the border between Scotland and England. He was a tall and most impressive man, and he came from a strongly medical background. There had been fifteen doctors in the family, including his father, George Hume, after whom the future Cardinal was called.

16

There had also been some clergymen among the Humes whose family religion was Anglican. George's father, William Errington Hume, followed the family tradition and studied medicine. In due course he became a very distinguished specialist in heart diseases. In the early part of the century, he was the first person to introduce the electro-cardiograph into the city of Newcastle. This is a machine by which the health of a patient's heart can be very accurately tested, and nowadays it is a routine feature of every hospital or clinic.

Had William stayed in Scotland during all his working life it is very doubtful if he would have married a Catholic. He would probably never have met any Catholics among the upper middle and 'professional' classes with whom he mostly mixed in the course of his social life. And even if he had met a Catholic girl, it is doubtful if he would have married her. Members of different religions kept themselves apart from each other and never — unlike modern times — visited each others churches.

However, with the outbreak of the First World War in 1914, William Hume, then aged thirty-five, volunteered for service as a consulting physician with the British Forces in France. His bravery was recognised and he was twice 'mentioned in despatches'. After the war he was given the honour of being made a Commander of the Order of St Michael and St George. It was while serving in France, at the base hospital at Boulogne, that he met Marie-Elizabeth Tisseyre. She was the daughter of a French army officer and had

First World War trenches

been evacuated to Boulogne from Lille in the path of the advancing German army. They fell in love and decided to get married as soon as possible, despite the fact that Marie-Elizabeth was seventeen years younger than Hume. They agreed to ignore the age-gap, and also their difference in religion, nationality and language.

Sir William Hume, as he was later called, never became a Catholic nor did he ever learn to speak French. His wife, a devout Roman Catholic, learned English but almost always spoke to the children in

French. This was a great advantage to young George in later years. But when their mother spoke French to them on the trams in Newcastle, the children — George, his three sisters and brother — were always a bit embarrassed! The family lived upstairs at number 4 Ellison Place in Newcastle and Sir William's consulting rooms were on the ground floor. There was plenty of room as it was a large eighteenth-century house, and, the Humes did not suffer directly from the 'depression' during the years between the wars. Instead, they lived comfortably and went abroad for their summer holidays, usually to the Normandy seaside in their mother's native France.

George was a cheerful child and often acted the clown in family pantomimes. But he also had a serious side to his nature. He was very observant and soon realised how much poverty there was within a few streets of the prosperous part of Newcastle where he and his family lived. In some of these streets he saw boys and girls of his own age with no shoes or stockings. In church he noticed that many of the women had to wear their husbands' caps as they had nothing else to cover their heads with. He found out that some of the families were living twelve to a room. 'I was forced to compare my own good fortune with theirs,' he was to say many years later. 'I think that childhood experience determined my way of life, oddly, to become a monk.'

There were of course other influences as well. As far as religion was concerned, this came chiefly from George's mother Lady Hume, and all the children were brought up very strictly in the Catholic faith. But in view of what was to happen to George in later life, it is important to know that young George also came into contact with the Church of England, to which his father belonged. A regular visitor to the house was a friend of George's father, the Rev. Henry Bates, then vicar of the Anglican parish church of Jesmond in Newcastle and afterwards Archdeacon of Lindisfarne. He quite often brought Holy Communion to Sir William Hume, as he came towards the end of his life. Young George Hume was therefore brought up in a home which was thoroughly Christian, where each parent, one Anglican, the other Roman Catholic, completely respected the particular branch of Christianity to which the other belonged. This kind of respect between different kinds of Christians was not so prevalent in England fifty years ago as it is today. Now, one of the greatest champions of such inter-religious respect — technically known as 'ecumenism' — is Cardinal Hume.

George's piety as a boy was natural and unaffected. His mother always wanted him to be a priest but the final decision on the matter (or rather the response that George was to make to a call from God, as he sees it) was to be entirely his own. George was still very young when he first felt this call to the priesthood. To begin with, he wanted to join an order of friars called the Dominicans. They took their name from their founder, Saint Dominic. A local priest who had taken George on some of his visits to poor families was a Dominican priest, and George had noticed the good work this priest was able to do among people who were unhappy. They were unhappy not just because they were poor, but because their great difficulties in life had made some of them give up all hope for the future. George felt that a deeper understanding of the consolations of religion could help such people regain hope. So he decided he was being led to the priesthood and wanted to be a Dominican.

All of this has a lot to do with what it means to have a 'calling' to be a clergyman, or priest, as it is often called. Throughout history thousands of men and women have felt that God has given them certain signs or signals that He would like them to serve Him in a special way. Such signals are not like signposts on a road. They are more likely to be something that someone says, the example of a teacher, or what you read in a book. If a person reads an exciting book about the adventures of arctic explorers, he may want to become an explorer himself. Similarly, if the book is about a holy person who has given up a lot to serve God by helping others, the person reading it may want to follow in the footsteps of such a 'hero'.

George still had this desire to be a Dominican when he first went away to boarding school. He was eleven at the time and the school he went to was about 130 kilometres away, in North Yorkshire. It was called Gilling, and was the preparatory school for the much bigger school of Ampleforth, which was only a short journey away. The two schools are separated by a shallow valley which looks very beautiful in the summer, but can be freezing in the winter. The buildings of Ampleforth College and Abbey are on the north side of the valley and can be very cold when the

Ampleforth College, Yorkshire

wind and snow arrive.

By the time George was thirteen, he had joined the senior school. He still wanted to be a priest, but was no longer so sure about being a Dominican. Ampleforth was, and still is, run by an order of monks called the Benedictines. The order was founded as long ago as the sixth century by a saintly man called Benedict, who was one of the most important figures in the whole of Christian history. It is not surprising that George Hume should be attracted by such a man, for Benedict was shy and unassuming but possessed of enormous inner strength and conviction. He was also very practical. He wrote a 'rule', which was intended to be an everyday guide to life for men who felt an urge to leave their homes and ordinary lives and to live together in devotion to God. That place would be

22

called a community, and the men would be called monks. Their daily life would be divided between prayer and work. The prayers would be said when they were alone in their little rooms, called cells, and also when they came together several times a day in church. Then their prayers would be sung. Later, this came to be called 'plainchant'. The work they would do might be farming, teaching, preaching, helping the poor and the sick, or any other similar sort of occupation.

If the monks were happy deep down in themselves, it was taken as a sign that they had a genuine calling from God. If they could find no such inner peace they were given a period of time to decide on their future. After a number of years, they could either leave the monastery, or take their final vows, which bound them to stay for ever under obedience to the leading monk, who was called the Abbot.

George Hume, the teenage schoolboy, thought about all these things very carefully. And he prayed hard to make the right final decision. Meanwhile he took an enthusiastic part in the usual school activities and was an outstandingly good sportsman. He was excellent at running and hurdling but perhaps shone most of all on the rugby field. He was a fast and feared rugby forward, a courageous and tough player and high scorer. Eventually he captained the Ampleforth Rugby XV.

At lessons he was good, but not always a top scorer. 'No fool', is perhaps the best and most accurate description of him at that time. More importantly, he was an excellent mixer and judge of people. He had a gift for friendship and showed himself to be a natural leader, particularly on the sports field.

Ampleforth College Rugby Captain 1940-41

3 The Big Decision

The ambitions for the future which George Hume had had since he was nine or ten never left him. They stayed with him all through his schooldays and became stronger as he got older. By the time he was eighteen, his conscience made him feel that nothing should be allowed to stand in the way of what he felt was a very clear call from God, and that he should take the first steps toward the priesthood. But obeying such a call is not easy. The temptation to use some external circumstance or human argument as an excuse not to take that first plunge is very strong indeed. In fact, the moral courage needed not to reject or postpone a definite call from God to serve him as a priest or nun is even greater than the kind of courage needed to face physical danger.

While writing this book I went to see Cardinal Hume and one of the questions I asked him was how would he sum up, all these years later, his thoughts about that big decision made by him just over forty years ago. What he said was this.

When I was quite young I realised that it was very important to do the best I could with my life. I was attracted first of all to being a priest and then to becoming a monk. Many of my friends who also wanted to do the best with their lives were attracted to follow other ways of life . . . I never thought I was doing anything other than answer a call from God to be a monk, just as I'm quite certain that my brother followed his own call from God to be a doctor. Sometimes people think that monks and nuns have gloomy lives. This is far from the truth. Their lives are generally busy and happy ones.

Yet, although it is quite true that the life of a priest or nun is happy, the early days of training are unquestionably very hard. This is particularly true in the case of someone who becomes a 'novice' in a monastery. A novice is a trainee, and the training period of two years puts the young man's ambition to become a monk to the severest kind of test. Becoming a soldier would be easier because even though army training is tough and testing, there are compensations such as periods of relief and relaxation with friends. These hardly exist in the case of a novice. He lives a life in which he is completely cut off from almost all the other members of the community. His only regular companions are the 'novice master' and his fellow novices, who may number anything from two to five in any one year.

The novice master is a wise man who realises that his novices must be prepared to be lonely, if they are to be true for the rest of their lives to that call which has come to them when still only in their teens. Although they will eventually mix again freely with men and

Novices at their studies

women of all kinds, they will in a sense always be alone. For one thing, in order to qualify for 'ordination' (being made a priest) they will be called upon to make a solemn vow to remain unmarried (technically called 'celibate') for the rest of their lives.

To bind yourself, when still so young, to give up the pleasure and companionship of marriage and children is not a step to be taken lightly. Many years after Basil Hume had become Abbot, he was to say to his monks.

Celibacy affects us in what is most intimate and personal deep down in each one of us. Unfortunately, it is no more possible for the young monk to foresee how it is going to affect him later in life than it is possible for the young married man to know how his state of life is going to work out for him.

Hume went on to say that not being married did not make a monk any less a man. He would still have to exercise manly virtues, while possessing the normal power to attract and be attracted by other people. But he could be consoled by remembering that his vow to remain unmarried was taken to imitate Jesus Christ himself.

No less important are the other vows the novice will eventually have to take: vows of poverty and obedience. The vow of poverty means that after ordination he will not be able to have any possessions of his own. Though each monk will be given enough for his daily needs, all money and other goods will be shared in a monastic community. As for the vow of obedience, this means that the 'fully professed' monk binds himself for ever to

28

The monastic life as a Benedictine monk

be obedient to his superior, the Abbot of his monastery. But of course, the vow is really made to God for after his period of trial is over, it is to God that the monk binds himself. But as far as he is concerned, he considers that God's voice on earth will be the voice, a very gentle one, of the Abbot.

The novice's life, then, is not very adventurous in the ordinary sense of the word. His life is very confined, almost like being voluntarily in prison, with a strictly regulated day divided between time alone in his cell, prayer and spiritual reading in the company of his fellow novices, and periods of exercise. However, he is not completely cut off from the other monks of the monastery because he joins them for the singing, in choir, of what is called the 'divine office'. It is called the

29

office because it is the *official* prayer of the church. Monks all over the world come together in their own church several times a day to sing God's praises through the ancient psalms and other traditional prayers. It is very beautiful to listen to, and the sight of about fifty or sixty monks, kneeling or standing and facing each other in their choir stalls while singing alternate verses of the songs and psalms, is an impressive one.

Once he had taken the plunge, Basil Hume, by which name he was now generally known, moved steadily forward in his new life. The period of being a novice is followed by several years devoted to the study of philosophy and theology as well as general studies, and may well include a course at university. Basil Hume went to St Benet's Hall, Oxford. He spent three happy and fruitful years studying history and obtained a good degree. He had by now made what is known as his 'simple profession' as a monk. This means that he had taken vows but the vows were not yet permanent.

After Oxford he went on for further studies in theology at the University of Fribourg in Switzerland. This was followed by ordination as a 'fully professed' monk when his vows were considered to be binding for ever. In 1950, he began a career as a teacher at his old school, Ampleforth, where he was also a member of Ampleforth's monastic community. This was to be the happiest period of his adult life. He enjoyed the rough-and-tumble of everyday school life and did not find that being a master stopped him from also being a friend and companion of the boys under his care.

In fact, as a junior monk he was not beyond taking

part in some fun and games himself occasionally. Once he and a friend pulled off a hoax by pretending to be parents who wanted to be shown over the school before sending their son there. They arrived disguised as a colonel and his wife. Fr Basil played the part of the colonel. He carried a walking stick and wore a large false moustache. At first everyone was completely taken in. The guest master was sent for to show these distinguished visitors round the school. Then they were invited to stay for tea. This turned out to be bad luck for Fr. Basil. As he sipped his tea, the steam from the hot cup began to melt the gum holding his false moustache in place. 'The game's up, Basil,' said the guest master. And that was that.

Fr. Basil proved to have a great gift for teaching. Though his manner was easy and relaxed, his old students, when asked about him, will say that he had a lifelong influence on them. In other words, he was more than just a teacher. He was a leader and a source of inspiration. His example and good humour proved to be a greater inspiration than the harsh teaching methods often preferred by other less successful teachers.

Quite soon he was appointed a housemaster. This meant that he was in charge of one of the 'houses', each of about eighty boys, into which the school is divided. All the houses at Ampleforth are called after some famous Benedictine saint. As a boy, Fr. Basil had been at St. Dunstan's. As a housemaster he was in charge of St. Bede's. He remained head of the languages department of the school but now had the added responsibility of caring for the spiritual and everyday lives of the boys in his house. He turned out to be very good at this. He had the courage to say what he thought, but did not hurt or upset any of the boys when he had to scold or correct them. They generally followed his advice because they admired him, especially on the sports field. Having been head of the rugby team as a boy, he now coached rugby very successfully, and continued to be active in other sports as well.

After a while he was given an extra job to do. He was put in charge of teaching theology to the young monks. Theology is the subject connected with God and the message of Christianity. Fr. Basil Hume's daily contact with the monks made him very popular with them. It was largely because of this that a big change came into his life in 1963, when he was forty years of age. The time had come to elect a new head of the whole community — that is a new Abbot. The previous Abbot had been doing the job for twenty-four years, having been twice re-elected. This would make life difficult for whoever was chosen to follow him. The choice fell on Basil Hume. It was big responsibility and Hume was naturally nervous of taking on such an awesome task.

But the monks' choice turned out to be a particularly good one. It came just at the time when all the Roman Catholic bishops of the world were gathering in Rome for what was called the Vatican Council. One of the main objectives of this enormous assembly, whose sittings lasted for four years, was to bring the Roman Catholic Church up-to-date. The bishops wanted to make the Church's centuries-old traditions more real

The Vatican, Rome

and urgent for Christians of the twentieth century.
Every aspect of the life of the Church, not least that of
monasteries and schools such as Ampleforth, were

33

affected by the findings of this great Council. Abbot
Basil Hume knew that a testing time lay ahead and, as
usual in such circumstances, he prayed for help and
guidance.

4 From Abbot to Archbishop

If you have ever been to the theatre, have you ever wondered what the actors backstage are whispering to each other as they wait for their cue? Perhaps they are commenting on something that has gone slightly wrong. A mistake can happen during a religious function too, as one did when Fr. Basil Hume, during an elaborate ceremony in the magnificent church of Ampleforth, was being solemnly installed as Abbot of the community.

Hume was saying High Mass, which is basically the same as an ordinary Mass except that much of it is sung instead of spoken. (Mass is the Catholic counterpart of the Anglican Eucharistic service.) It was an emotional occasion for the new Abbot. He was not yet used to the honour and the heavy responsibility of his new office. And so, when he was reciting the Our Father during the Mass he completely broke down the words 'Thy will be done'. There was a painful silence which seemed longer than it really was. One of the Abbot's fellow monks standing nearby sidled up to the new Abbot and hissed in a stage whisper, 'Get on with it, get on with it!' The faltering Abbot was jolted back to reality and firmly pronounced the words 'Thy will be done!'

As Abbot, he carried out what he felt to be God's will with the utmost care and conscientiouness. But prudently he did so on a day-to-day basis. He met each day with renewed resolution, rather than try to plan far ahead to make success of his 'reign' as Abbot. In other words he met each problem as he came to it, all the time building up his own confidence and that of the 125 monks under his care, with just enough forward planning to deal with the most urgent needs of his community. He was only indirectly concerned with the running of Ampleforth school which has its own headmaster.

Teaching is not the only work done by the monks. Many work away from the boundaries of the monastery as parish priests and even as missionaries; an offshoot of Ampleforth, called a Priory, had been established as far away as St Louis, in the United States of America. This too came under the care of Abbot Hume, who had to spend quite a lot of time travelling.

Basil Hume was Abbot of Ampleforth for thirteen years, having been elected to a second term of office in 1971. He has been called a great Abbot, partly because of his considerable success in steering his large and important community so well through a period of great change in the Catholic Church. Many of the older monks, for example, did not like the change from Latin to English as the language in which they were now to sing the praises of the Lord. They felt that something they considered beautiful and helpful to their devotion should not be cast aside. Hume's great strength was his willingness to listen with love to the worries of

36

everyone. He always had time for everyone and never imposed his own will on others. He maintained his authority over the monastery by what one member of the community called his gift for keeping up a personal relationship of 'confidence and affection'.

But Basil Hume suffered inwardly a great deal during the later part of his time as Abbot. He underwent a severe trial which comes to many priests, especially the best and most devout ones. He had great difficulty in continuing to believe in what he was doing and even in the God to whom he had dedicated his life.

To have such a difficulty is something like having a nervous breakdown since the person feels tired out and very depressed. But with the help of prayer and his own courage Abbot Hume overcame this ordeal. A fellow monk later said that he thought that this trial was a preparation for the even greater responsibility of being Archbishop of Westminster. 'Some of the radiance of Basil now,' he added, 'is that of a man who has gone through darkness into light.' Basil Hume, after he had safely made this hard journey from 'darkness into light', was a happier man than ever in the early seventies. Ampleforth, as was clear to any visitor at that time, reflected the happiness, faith and optimism of its Abbot.

Like the rest of the Catholics in England and Wales, Ampleforth was sad to hear of the death of Cardinal Heenan, Archbishop of Westminster, on 6 November 1976. Soon afterwards, the Pope's representative to the Catholic Church in Britain, who had the title of the 'Apostolic Delegate,' began making enquiries among

Catholic clergy and others as to whose name he should submit to the Pope for appointment as Westminster's next Archbishop. Nearly everyone assumed that the choice would fall on someone who was already a Bishop of some other diocese. This had been the custom for many years. But when some weeks passed without anybody's name clearly emerging as leading candidate for the vacancy, all sorts of rumours began to arise. Perhaps the choice would not fall on a man who was already a Bishop after all?

Meanwhile, Abbot Hume, whose name had been mentioned in the rumours, left Ampleforth on 2 February to attend a study course for senior Church leaders at St George's House, Windsor. On the evening of 5 February he went to have dinner with an old school friend called Colonel (later Sir John) Johnston, who worked for the Queen in the Royal Household and lived in a house in the Home Park at Windsor. They had just sat down to dinner and were finishing their soup when Abbot Hume was told he was wanted urgently on the telephone. It was the Apostolic Delegate saying that he wanted Fr. Basil to call on him on the Saturday of that week. The Abbot knew what this meant and turned pale. He later confessed that he did not enjoy the rest of the meal and had a poor night. He knew that the Pope had chosen him to be Westminster's next Archbishop. The Apostolic Delegate confirmed this when they met a few days later, although the appointment had to be kept secret for ten days.

They were ten extremely difficult days for Abbot Hume! But the secret was kept and the official announcement, on 17 February, caused a sensation. Hume's name was not yet at all well known, even to Catholics. Journalists had to make a quick study of this previously unknown man, who had become famous overnight. The fact that he was a sportsman seemed to interest them almost more than anything else. This was reflected in the next morning's headlines, such as: Sporty monk is new RC leader; Sportsman in the shoes of the Cardinal; Soccer fan monk new Archbishop; and Rugby ace is new Catholic Leader. Most Catholics were taken by surprise, but within a very short time all of them realised what an inspired choice it had been.

Abbot Hume was installed as Archbishop of Westminster on 25 March, which turned out to be an historic day both for the Church of England and for the Roman Catholic Church in this country. This was because it was not only the day of the former Abbot's ordination as a Bishop and installment as Archbishop of Westminster at Westminster Cathedral; it was also the day on which Benedictine monks from all over England, especially from Ampleforth, sang solemn vespers in Latin at the great Anglican church of Westminster Abbey. The new Archbishop of Westminster had received an invitation from the Dean of Westminster for him and monks of his order to attend this service as a mark of the friendship between the two churches. It was a unique occasion, and another important step towards eventual unity between Anglicanism and Roman Catholicism. And indeed, Archbishop Hume has long been a great friend of the present Archbishop of Canterbury, Dr. Runcie. They

Cardinal Basil's friend, Dr Runcie, Archbishop of Canterbury consult each other frequently on matters of common Christian concern.

When addressing the huge congregation at Westminster Abbey on that day in March, Archbishop Hume said, 'I have spoken in a great Church of the Anglican Communion. But the Catholic Church wishes to speak and to listen to all Churches, to all men of all religions or of none.' These stirring words followed an appeal to heed with care words spoken by the Pope himself (Paul VI) who had said, 'The Roman Catholic Church — this humble "Servant of the Servants of God" — is able to embrace her ever beloved Sister (the Anglican Church) in the one authentic Communion of the Family of Christ.'

5   Hume for Pope?

Archbishop Basil Hume, who was created a Cardinal by the Pope in May 1976, soon became one of the most familiar figures in Britain, often being seen on television and heard on the radio. He made many courageous pronouncements on public matters. At the beginning, however, he knew hardly any of the priests or people in his huge new diocese. In his job, this was a great disadvantage. He overcame it by facing the challenge head on and in a remarkably short time came to know and be known by all of his priests and hundreds of the people living in the Westminster diocese. He was soon recognised as the most popular prelate ever to have been Archbishop of Westminster. He achieved this reputation by being, as one observer called him 'a gentle and dedicated reformer'. In this respect he reminded many people of the most popular Pope of modern times, Pope John XXIII.

Perhaps his greatest achievement in his first two years was to make his people happy Christians, much happier than many of them had been in the past. Previously, Catholics had got rather used to being told about the things they must *not* do. Cardinal Hume encouraged them in the things they must and could do to become happier and more fulfilled Christians. Young people flocked to Archbishop's House where he held 'open house' on Saturday evenings about once a month. At these informal gatherings the Cardinal came across brilliantly as a man who is both holy and human. His fame spread far and wide and, in the early part of 1978, he was being spoken of as a possible future Pope!

It is not easy to account for this sudden enormous popularity. Basil Hume is not a man given to making grand gestures or dramatic speeches. But he did so many kind and considerate things that gradually more and more people began to realise what a truly unusual, inspiring, and above all genuine, man he was. There are dozens of examples, but, let one suffice for the moment.

In July 1978, there was an outcry about the unjust trials in Russia of two prominent Jews. A twenty-four hour protest vigil was organised to take place outside the Russian Embassy in London in protest against the trials. One night, Cardinal Hume arrived to join the demonstrators and to give them words of encouragement. Commenting on his unexpected appearance, Linda Isaacs, one of the organisers, said 'We were honoured and delighted to see Cardinal Hume – he arrived with no pomp and circumstance at all'.

Meanwhile the Cardinal went about his many duties, not listening to the people who said he might be considered a possible candidate for Pope. Then, on 8 August, 1978, the Pope who had appointed Hume to Westminster, Paul VI, died. As it is one of the duties of all Cardinals to elect a new Pope, Cardinal Hume was

Cardinal Basil Hume with his Holiness Pope Paul VI

soon journeying to Rome to take part in the election.
But he did not believe that he could possibly be elected
Pope himself. However, he was taken aback when, on
his arrival, he discovered that he appeared to be the
favourite choice of many Cardinals, including the
powerful group from the USA. Archbishop Roach,
President of the American Bishops, publicly stated that
'a very strong evangeliser' was needed and that
Cardinal Hume was just such a man.

In the end, however, the choice fell upon the
Patriarch of Venice, Cardinal Luciani. He was elected
on 26 August and took the name of Pope John Paul I.
With his warm, ready smile, he instantly captured

people's hearts. But tragedy was to follow. Thirty-three days later the new Pope was found dead in bed.

His death was a tremendous shock for the whole world, not just the Catholic Church. Among other things, it meant that the Cardinals, who had only just got home, had to set off once more for Rome to elect another man as Pope. This time the rumours were even stronger that the choice would fall for the first time for hundreds of years on a non-Italian. Once again, Cardinal Hume's name was brought into the running, though he himself did everything he could to scotch any such idea. His most widely quoted words at the time were about the Pope who had just died, 'We are left with the memory of a humble man who radiated joy and serenity in his engaging smile'.

In discussing this extraordinary period in the recent history of the Papacy and Catholic Church, Cardinal Hume said to me;

In 1978 all the Cardinals in the world came together twice to elect the Pope. I remember coming out of the Vatican after the first election and saying to someone, 'What a marvellous experience!' But I hoped it would not be repeated in my lifetime. So I was full of gloom when, a month later, we had to start all over again and ended up by electing the present Pope. I felt as I have described because it is a heavy responsibility to elect the head of the Church and I can assure you that during the conclave the Vatican could not get any good ratings as a hotel! But electing a Pope is a great spiritual experience because I truly felt the presence of God. Remember that we were totally cut off from the outside world — no letters, telephone, newspapers, transistors, television, etc . . .

It cannot be denied that when, on the morning of 12 October 1978, Cardinal Hume entered the enclosed surroundings of the 'conclave' in the Vatican to elect a new Pope, he was a worried man. ('Conclave' is a word taken from Latin meaning a place 'locked with a key' where the Cardinals are kept until they have decided on the new man to be Bishop of Rome, and leader of the Catholic Church.) The Cardinal was accompanied to the Vatican that morning by a close friend and there were some emotional scenes outside the great door where other Cardinals were embracing their friends and saying goodbye. Some of them seemed to be acting as if they might be elected Pope. By contrast, Cardinal Hume's handshake with his friend was relaxed and matter-of-fact. The Cardinal has never divulged what his thoughts were while in the conclave as he strongly believes in keeping the promise of silence about all that goes on while a Pope is being elected.

The choice fell this time on a Polish Cardinal called Karol Wojtyla who took the name of John Paul II. This Pope was destined to do a lot of travelling, but little did anyone think that one of the places he would visit would be Great Britain. But that was in the future. With the excitement of a non-Italian Pope now ruling the Church and the exhaustion of two visits in a short time to Rome, Cardinal Hume returned gratefully to London to take up again his daily routine as

Archbishop of Westminster. We should now have a quick look at what that daily routine usually involves.

His Holiness Pope Jonh Paul II

6 All in a Day's Work

So let us take a glimpse at a typical day in the working life of Cardinal Hume. Although he has to go out of England quite a lot, especially because of duties in Rome, the majority of his time is spent in London. His day is long and hard but, in the way in which he himself describes it, it sounds calm and unhurried. Unlike most of us, he does not get up at the last possible moment, just in time to scramble to school or work. Instead, he sets his alarm for 6 am. Too early for comfort you might say. But the Cardinal does not mind too much — for two reasons. First, he has been used to getting up even earlier for many years. This is the custom in monasteries, and Ampleforth is no exception. Second, he happens to like bells. Bells attract him — even those of telephones — because he hears them, in his own words, as 'a summons to help others'. Even so, he sometimes tries to steal another ten minutes in bed. But, one way or another, he is down in his private chapel by 6.30. There he spends three-quarters of an hour alone in prayer.

Such solitary prayer is a very important part of the life of anyone who has dedicated his or her life to God. Perhaps surprisingly, most of the prayer consists of thoughts rather than words. Its purpose is to try and establish a two-way channel of communication between God and the person who is praying. But how difficult that is! Even the greatest saints and mystics found it hard. It does not consist of rattling off a set formula taken from a book or learned by heart. It depends more on establishing, day by day, an intimate relationship with God and talking to Him as a friend. Having talked, the person praying may then try to 'listen'. He or she will not, of course, hear voices, but may well find a response from God through his or her own thoughts and emotions. To receive such a response, prayer must take place every day. It is no good to try just every now and again. After making the effort every day for many years, the results, at least on *some* days if not all, will be successful and helpful to the person praying. Part of the training of someone like Cardinal Hume has been in the mysterious art, or gift from God, of praying. Constant practice makes it, if never easy, at least less difficult as the years go by.

Furthermore, the Christian church has always taught that it is best to pray first thing in the morning. Cardinal Hume agrees with this. While admitting that 'prayer is seldom easy,' he confesses that 'it has a lot to do with how tired I am, or how peaceful. I don't find it easy at the end of a long day . . .' During his time as Abbot, the Cardinal often had to speak about prayer to the members of his community. What he said was found very helpful and much of it has been put into book form and read by thousands of people.

When talking to the Cardinal during the writing of

this book, I asked him if he could explain how prayer can bring someone close to a God whom no-one can see or hear. This is what he said;

I was once playing hide and seek with a little girl aged ten and a boy of seven. I can remember that at one point the girl hid in a cupboard under the stairs. It was full of junk and had no light. I got to her hiding place first. But we then had to sit very quietly not talking to each other so as not to give the hiding place away to the little boy. I remember sitting in the dark with the little girl, knowing that she was there, happy to be in her presence, but we couldn't see each other owing to the need for silence, and couldn't hear each other, there being no light. . . . Sometimes in prayer we just *know* in a strange way that God is very close. We do not see him because we haven't got the right kind of light; and we don't hear him because he hasn't got a voice like ours. We just know he's there and we're happy to be with him, and he with us.

At about 7.15, the Cardinal is joined in the little chapel by the small group of nuns who look after the house. They say together a prayer called 'Lauds', which is a prayer used by the Church for many centuries to give morning praise to God. At 7.30 he says Mass, the Catholic Church's principal act of worship. But one of his engagements later in the day may well be to visit one of the many parishes in the area under his control, which is called his 'diocese'. In that case he will postpone saying Mass until he reaches the parish

Cardinal Basil greets HRH The Queen

church in question, and use the time saved, between 7.30 and 8, to write a speech or sermon.

Over breakfast at eight he reads *The Times* and then *The Guardian*. By 8.30 at the latest, he is at his desk. His work load is very heavy as he gets an enormous amount of letters, all of which he opens himself and reads with care. Replies are dictated almost immediately and people invariably find their letters to the Cardinal are answered by return of post. He says he gets mainly two

51

kinds of letters — 'Hurrah' letters and 'Boo' letters. Naturally, he does not like getting 'Boo' letters, but makes a point of writing a nice letter back. To his surprise he sometimes finds that this results in a friendly and understanding letter in return.

Paperwork at his desk can take him the whole morning, but he often has to break off at 11 or 11.30 to receive visitors. Dozens of people every month want to see the Cardinal about something, and he never refuses their requests. Lunch is at 1 p.m., and especially in his first years as Archbishop of Westminster, the Cardinal found this a useful time to get to know the priests of his diocese. There are around five hundred of them altogether. He would invite five or six of them to lunch about three days a week and soon got to know all his priests personally. To keep in touch, he also gave them a private telephone number which they could use to ring him up any time of the day or night if they needed advice or help. He soon became a trusted friend and leader of these hard-worked men who, in the scattered parishes they served, looked after the spiritual lives of thousands of people.

After lunch, the Cardinal always tries to take some form of exercise. He is a tall, wiry man who has long thrived on fresh air and athletics. He usually takes a vigorous walk, and until 1983 he used to jog and play squash when an operation to replace his left hip made these activities impossible for a while. In the late afternoon, the Cardinal often has to see more visitors and on most evenings he goes out to visit one of the many parishes in his diocese. 'Usually by 5.30 p.m., I'm

Cardinal Hume and friend

away to engagements. It's a good time for visiting
parishes because people can only come after work . . .'
These visits by Cardinal Hume have been hugely
successful. No-one, of whatever age, ever seems to feel
shy with him. He loves talking to people and they love
talking to him. He has a valuable gift of using simple
words in his speeches and sermons, but, coming from
him, they are words which make a deep impression on

his listeners. They are not easily forgotten. He particularly likes, and is liked by young people and his many visits to schools are always happy occasions for all concerned. No less successful are his many visits to hospitals, prisons, orphanages; and to the sick and elderly in their own homes, or homes for the old and disabled.

Parish visits may go on until quite late, or else the Cardinal may sometimes have to go elsewhere for his evening meal. This is yet another way to meet members of his huge 'flock' and to keep in touch with interesting people and important events. He reluctantly has to refuse many invitations because of lack of time.

He likes to be home by 10 p.m., when he will put on an old sweater and, if he has not eaten earlier, have a sandwich and coffee while looking at the late news on television. 'I'm not a telly fan,' he says, 'but I like to watch *Match of the Day* — that's a rule of the house!'

Obviously not every day in the Cardinal's busy and varied life is exactly like that just described. He spends a lot of time travelling and has to refuse more invitations to make speeches and attend important occasions than he is able to accept. For example, as president of the Council of Conferences for European Bishops, which deals with the affairs of twenty-three countries (including those of Eastern Europe) he has to make many trips to the Continent.

Among his many frequent visits to the USA, perhaps the most notable was in 1982 when he gave the opening speech each day at a week-long combined conference-retreat for all the Bishops of the USA. It was the first time that all these Bishops had been gathered together under one roof. The event took place at St John's College, Minnesota, the largest Benedictine monastery in the world. During the conference it was announced that Diana, Princess of Wales, had given birth to a son. So, at the conclusion of the conference the American Bishops gave Cardinal Hume a memorable and unusual gift. It was a T-shirt inscribed with the words 'It's a boy'.

7   The Future?

In trying to give some idea of what Cardinal Hume is like as a person, I have not left myself much space to give a detailed description of all his activities in the eight years that he has been Archbishop Westminster. This will have to be left to future historians. In this kind of book, it seems more important to let Basil Hume's character come across in another way: by describing, for example, his reaction to first becoming a Cardinal after which he soon won so many hearts; by quoting his own words on the same kind of situations and problems that we all have to face; and by mentioning the important part he played in making possible the Pope's visit to Britain and acting as the Holy Father's principal host. But one should also ask a final question about the future, since Cardinal Hume almost certainly has much unfinished work to complete.

One man who worked closely with the Cardinal in his first years at Westminster stresses Hume's informality, which helps everyone around him to relax, even when very important duties are to be performed. The next thing that strikes those around the Cardinal is that his own very strong faith had to be 'hewn out' of earlier difficulties, just as you must sometimes dig a very deep foundation through hard and rocky ground if you want to build a house that will stand the strains of time. The Cardinal has suffered in holding on to his personal faith. Now it is all the stronger and he is better fitted to bolster the faith of others.

He is sensitive to minor as well as major causes of unhappiness. I knew one almost inconsolable lady, who had lost her only daughter, but found a consolation she could never have believed possible after a visit to Cardinal Hume. As it happens, she was not a Catholic. At the other end of the scale, the Cardinal was once making one of his visits to a school. Overcome by the emotion of the occasion, a little girl burst into tears. Cardinal Hume told her, 'That's how I often feel!' The little girl was soon smiling.

But the burden of his new job as Archbishop was at first daunting, even 'battering,' as one person described it. It took its toll on the Cardinal, but he gradually grew into the job, praying daily that he might never disappoint those under his care. He never has. He has inspired trust as few other Catholic leaders in Britain have ever done. He looks everyone straight in the eye and shows that during the time they are talking to each other, be it even for only a few seconds, all his attention is on and with that person. He is not a showman. He is not a superstar. He is a *person*, and this, in a word, is perhaps the key to his astonishing success.

But what happens when some tragedy hits him? How does he react to adversity? What are his thoughts, for example, on the death of others?

Cardinal Basil as he is today, ninth Archbishop of Westminster

I have always, he told me, been saddened by the death of people who have meant a great deal to me. Everyone has that experience. The more you love a person the more you grieve. As we come to understand more and more that there is another life after death, then the pain of parting is softened. But it is not completely removed.

What are his reactions to the good things in life? Of these he says;

I've always enjoyed certain things in life and on the whole they've been rather ordinary and simple things. For instance I've always enjoyed playing any kind of game even when not particularly good at it. And I've always enjoyed the company of good friends. I find that I forget too easily to thank God for these things. And I know that it is important to be grateful for the happy days . . .

One of the happiest occasions was the visit of the Pope to Britain in June 1982. Because of possible political difficulties arising from Britain's war with Argentina over the Falklands, it was feared that the visit might have to be called off at the last moment. Cardinal Hume flew to Rome with the Roman Catholic Archbishop of Liverpool, Archbishop Worlock, and there met and prayed with some of the highest ranking prelates of the Church from Argentina. This showed how Christian love must try to cross political frontiers and help people on either side to understand each other better. Thus the Pope was able to come to Britain — afterwards visiting Argentina as well — and his visit here was a tremendous success. A large part of the credit for its success must go to Cardinal Hume who had never stopped hoping and praying that the visit would be able to take place. There is no room here to describe the details of that historic occasion but here is what Cardinal Hume says in thinking back on it;

I remember the extraordinary thrill that I got when I

accompanied the Pope to the field at Wembley. The great roar that came from the crowd to greet him and the singing that followed will always remain in my memory. The Pope had captured the hearts of that great crowd. And this happened wherever he went.

But what of the future? Will the Church continue to play an important part in our lives? Or will the world become empty of faith? It seems to depend on the kind of people we are. Perhaps these words of a humble and deep thinking, holy, yet humorous and humane man, will point the way, Cardinal Hume said,

For me there are two kinds of people. One kind can only see clouds on the horizon and so thinks that we are heading for disaster; the other kind sees, as the expression goes, the silver lining on these clouds. I believe that it is important to realise that we must always play our part to make the world a better place for everyone. But that can only happen when the hearts of people turn from cruelty and hatred to love and kindness.